THE ESKIMO TWINS by Lucy Fitch Perkins

Lucy Fitch Perkins was forty-eight when she was approached by a publisher friend who, impressed by her talents as both an illustrator and writer, which he knew through correspondence, urged her to write. He was so earnest that she thought of an idea for a children's book the next morning, and she immediately set to work making sketches and preparing the idea for presentation. The publisher came to dinner at their house the next evening and she showed him the idea. His response was immediate "go ahead and write it, and I want it". That book was The Dutch Twins, the first in what became a long running and wildly popular series. Here we publish another in the series 'The Eskimo Twins'.

Index Of Contents

INTRODUCTION - THE ESKIMO TWINS

This is the true story of Menie and Monnie and their two little dogs, Nip and Tup.

Menie and Monnie are twins, and they live far away in the North, near the very edge.

They are five years old.

Menie is the boy, and Monnie is the girl. But you cannot tell which is Menie and which is Monnie, not even if you look ever so hard at their pictures!

That is because they dress alike.

When they are a little way off even their own mother can't always tell. And if she can't, who can?

Sometimes the twins almost get mixed up about it themselves. And then it is very hard to know which is Nip and which is Tup, because the little dogs are twins too.

Nobody was surprised that the little dogs were twins, because dogs often are.

But everybody in the whole village where Menie and Monnie live was simply astonished to see twin babies!

They had never known of any before in their whole lives.

Old Akla, the Angakok, or Medicine Man of the village, shook his head when he heard about them. He said, "Such a thing never happened here before. Seals and human beings never have twins! There's magic in this."

The name of the twins' father was Kesshoo. If you say it fast it sounds just like a sneeze.

Their mother's name was Koolee. Kesshoo and Koolee, and Menie and Monnie, and Nip and Tup, all live together in the cold Arctic winter in a little stone hut, called an "igloo."

In the summer they live in a tent, which they call a "tupik." The winters are very long and cold, and what do you think! They have one night there that is four whole months long!

For four long months, while we are having Thanksgiving, and Christmas, and even Lincoln's Birthday, the twins never once see the sun!

But at last one day in early spring the sun comes up again out of the sea, looks at the world for a little while, and then goes out of sight again. Each day he stays for a longer time until after a while he doesn't go out of sight at all!

Then there are four long months of daylight when there is never any bedtime. Menie and Monnie just go to sleep whenever they feel sleepy.

Although many Eskimos think twins bring bad luck, Kesshoo and Koolee were very glad to have two babies.

They would have liked it better still if Monnie had been a boy, too, because boys grow up to hunt and fish and help get food for the family.

But Kesshoo was the best hunter and the best kyak man in the whole village. So he said to Koolee, "I suppose there must be girls in the world. It is no worse for us than for others."

So because Kesshoo was a brave fisherman and strong hunter, and because Koolee was clever in making clothing and shoes out of the skins of the animals which he brought home, the twins had the very best time that little Eskimo children can have.

And that is quite a good time, as you will see if you read all about it in this book.

I. THE TWINS GO COASTING

I.

One spring morning, very early, while the moon still shone and every one else in the village was asleep, Menie and Monnie crept out of the dark entrance of their little stone house by the sea.

The entrance to their little stone house was long and low like a tunnel. The Twins were short and fat. But even if they were short they could not stand up straight in the tunnel.

So they crawled out on all fours. Nip and Tup came with them. Nip and Tup were on all fours, too, but they had run that way all their lives, so they could go much faster than the twins. They got out first.

Then they ran round in circles in the snow and barked at the moon. When Menie and Monnie came out of the hole, Tup jumped up to lick Monnie's face. He bumped her so hard that she fell right into the snowbank by the entrance.

Monnie didn't mind a bit. She just put her two fat arms around Tup, and they rolled over together in the snow.

Monnie had on her fur suit, with fur hood and mittens, and it was hard to tell which was Monnie and which was Tup as they tumbled in the snow together.

Pretty soon Monnie picked herself up and shook off the snow. Then Tup shook himself, too. Menie was rolling over and over down the slope in front of the little stone house. His head was between his knees and his hands held his ankles, so he rolled just like a ball.

Nip was running round and round him and barking with all his might. They made strange shadows on the snow in the moonlight.

Monnie called to Menie. Menie straightened himself out at the bottom of the slope, picked himself up and ran back to her.

"What shall we play?" said Monnie.

"Let's get Koko, and go to the Big Rock and slide downhill," said Menie.

"All right," said Monnie. "You run and get your sled."

Menie had a little sled which his father had made for him out of driftwood. No other boy in the village had one. Menie's father had searched the beach for many miles to find driftwood to make this sled.

The Eskimos have no wood but driftwood, and it is so precious that it is hardly ever used for anything but big dog sledges or spears, or other things which the men must have.

Most of the boys had sleds cut from blocks of ice. Menie's sled was behind the igloo. He ran to get it, and then the twins and the pups, all four, started for Koko's house.

Koko's house was clear at the other end of the village. But that was not far away, for there were only five igloos in the whole town.

First there was the igloo where the twins lived. Next was the home of Akla, the Angakok, and his two wives. Then there were two igloos where several families lived together. Last of all was the one where Koko and his father and mother and baby brother lived.

Koko was six. He was the twins' best friend.

II.

The air was very still. There was not a sound anywhere except the barking of the pups, the voices of Menie and Monnie, and the creaking sound of the snow under their feet as they ran.

The round moon was sailing through the deep blue sky and shining so bright it seemed almost as light as day.

There was one window in each igloo right over the tunnel entrance, and these windows shone with a dull yellow light.

In front of the village lay the sea. It was covered with ice far out from shore. Beyond the ice was the dark water out of which the sun would rise by and by.

There was nothing else to be seen in all the twins' world. There were no trees, no bushes even; nothing but the white earth, the shadows of the rocks and the snow-covered igloos, the bright windows, and the moon shining over all.

III.

Menie and Monnie soon reached Koko's igloo. Menie and Nip got there first. Monnie came puffing along with Tup just a moment after.

Then the twins dropped on their hands and knees in front of Koko's hut, and stuck their heads into the tunnel. Nip and Tup stuck their heads in, too.

They all four listened. There was not a sound to be heard except loud snores! The snores came rattling through the tunnel with such a frightful noise that the twins were almost scared.

"They sleep out loud, don't they?" whispered Monnie.

"Let's wake them up," Menie whispered back.

Then the twins began to bark. "Ki-yi, ki-yi, ki-yi, ki-yi," just like little dogs!

Nip and Tup began to yelp, too. The snores and the yelps met in the middle of the tunnel and the two together made such a dreadful sound that Koko woke up at once. When he heard four barks he knew right away that it must be the twins and the little dogs.

So he stuck his head into the other end of the tunnel and called, "Keep still. You'll wake the baby! I'll be there in a minute."

Very soon Koko popped out of the black hole. He was dressed in a fur suit and mittens just like the twins.

IV.

The three children went along together toward the Big Rock. Monnie rode on the sled, and Menie and Koko pulled it. The Big Rock was very straight up and down on one side, and long and slanting on the other. The twins were going to coast down the slanting side.

They climbed to the top, and Menie had the first ride. He coasted down on his stomach with his little reindeer-skin kamiks (shoes) waving in the air.

Next Koko had a turn. What do you think he did? He stood straight up on the sled with the leather cord in his hand, and slid down that way! But then, you see, he was six.

When Monnie's turn came she wanted to go down that way, too. But Menie said, "No. You'd fall off and bump your nose! You have hardly any nose as it is, and you'd better save it!"

"I have as much nose as you have, anyway," said Monnie.

"Mine is bigger! I'm a boy!" said Menie.

Koko measured their noses with his finger.

"They are just exactly alike," he said.

Monnie turned hers up at Menie and said, "What did I tell you?"

Menie never said another word about noses. He just changed the subject. He said, "Let's all slide down at once."

Koko and Menie sat down on the sled. Monnie sat on Menie. Then they gave a few hitches to the sled and off they went.

Whiz! How they flew!

The pups came running after them. In some places where it was very slippery the pups coasted, too! But they did not mean to. They did not like it. The sled was almost at the end of the slide when it struck a piece of ice. It flew around sideways and spilled all the children in the snow.

Just then Nip and Tup came sliding along behind them. They couldn't stop, so there they all were in a heap together, with the dogs on top!

Menie rolled over and sat up in the snow. He was holding on to the end of his nose. "Iyi, iyi!" he howled, "I bumped my nose on a piece of ice!"

Monnie sat up in the snow, too. She pointed her fur mitten at Menie's nose and laughed. "Don't you know you haven't much nose?" she said. "You ought to be more careful of it!"

Koko kicked his feet in the air and laughed at Menie, and the little dogs barked. Menie thought he'd better laugh, too. He had just let go of his nose to begin when all of a sudden the little dogs stopped barking and stood very still!

Their hair stood up on their necks and they began to growl!

"Hark, the dogs see something," said Menie.

Monnie and Koko stopped laughing and listened. They could not hear anything. They could not see anything. Still Nip and Tup growled. The twins and Koko were children of brave hunters, so, although they were scared, they crept very quietly to the side of the Big Rock and peeped over.

Just that minute there was a dreadful growl! "Woof!" It was very loud, and very near, and down on the beach a shadow was moving! It was the shadow of a great white BEAR!

He was looking for fish and was cross because everything was frozen, and he could not find any on the beach.

The moment they saw him, the twins and Koko turned and ran for home as fast as ever their short legs could go! They did not even stop to get the precious sled. They just ran and ran.

Nip and Tup ran, too, with their ears back and their little tails stuck straight out behind them!

If they had looked back, they would have seen the bear stand up on his hind legs and look after them, then get down on all fours and start toward the Big Rock on a run.

But neither the children nor the little dogs looked back! They just ran with all their might until they reached the twins' igloo. Then they all dived into the tunnel like frightened rabbits.

V.

When they came up in the one little room of the igloo at the other end of the tunnel Kesshoo and Koolee were just crawling out of the warm fur covers of their bed. Menie and Monnie and Koko and the little dogs all began to talk at once.

The moment the twins' father and mother heard the word – bear – they jumped off the sleeping-bench and began to put on their clothes.

They both wore fur trousers and long kamiks, with coats of fur, so they looked almost as much alike in their clothes as the twins did in theirs.

The mother always wore her hair in a topknot on top of her head, tied with a leather thong. But now she wanted to make the bear think she was a man, too, so she pulled it down and let it hang about her face, just as her husband did.

In two minutes they were ready. Then the father reached for his lance, the mother took her knife, and they all crawled out of the tunnel.

The father went first, then the mother, then the three children and the pups. At the opening of the tunnel the father stopped, and looked all around to see if the bear were near.

The dogs in the village knew by this time that some strange animal was about, and the moment Kesshoo came out into the moonlight and started for the Big Rock, all the dogs ran, too, howling like a pack of wolves.

Kesshoo shouted back to his wife, "There really is a bear! I see him by the Big Rock; call the others."

So she sent Monnie into the igloo of the Angakok, and Menie and Koko into the next huts. She herself screamed, "A bear! A bear!" into the tunnel of Koko's hut.

The people in the houses had heard the dogs bark and were already awake. Soon they came pouring out of their tunnels armed with knives and lances. The women had all let down their hair, just as the twins' mother did. Each one carried her knife.

They all ran toward the Big Rock, too. Far ahead they could see the bear, and the dogs bounding along, and Kesshoo running with his lance in his hand.

Then they saw the dogs spring upon the bear. The bear stood up on his hind legs and tried to catch the dogs and crush them in his arms. But the dogs were too nimble. The bear could not catch them.

When Kesshoo came near, the bear gave a great roar, and started for him. The brave Kesshoo stood still with his lance in his hand, until the bear got quite near. Then he ran at the bear and plunged the lance into his side. The lance pierced the bear's heart. He groaned, fell to the ground, rolled over, and was still.

Then how everybody ran! Koko's mother had her baby in her hood, where Eskimo mothers always carry their babies. She could not run so fast as the others. The Angakok was fat, so he could not keep up, but he waddled along as fast as he could.

"Hurry, hurry," he called to his wives. "Bespeak one of his hind legs for me."

Menie and Monnie and Koko had such short legs they could not go very fast either, so they ran along with the Angakok, and Koko's mother, and Nip and Tup.

When they reached the bear they found all the other people crowded around it. Each one stuck his fingers in the bear's blood and then sucked his fingers. This was because they wanted all bears to know how they longed to kill them. As each one tasted the blood he called out the part of the bear he would like to have.

The wives of the Angakok cried, "Give a hind leg to the Angakok."

"The kidneys for Koko," cried Koko's mother when she stuck in her finger. "That will make him a great bear-hunter when he is big."

"And I will have the skin for the twins' bed," said their mother.

Kesshoo promised each one the part he asked for. An Eskimo never keeps the game he kills for himself alone. Every one in the village has a share.

The bear was very large. He was so large that though all the women pulled together they could not drag the body back to the village. The men laughed at them, but they did not help them.

So Koolee ran back for their sledge and harnesses for the dogs. Koko and Menie helped her catch the dogs and hitch them to the sledge.

It took some time to catch them for the dogs did not want to work. They all ran away, and Tooky, the leader of the team, pretended to be sick! Tooky was the mother of Nip and Tup, and she was a very clever dog. While Koolee and Koko and Menie were getting the sledge and dog-team ready, the rest of the women set to work with their queer crooked knives to take off the bear's skin. The moon set, and the sky was red with the colors of the dawn before this was done.

At last the meat was cut in pieces and Kesshoo and Koko's father held the dogs while the women heaped it on the sledge. The dogs wanted the meat. They jumped and howled and tried to get away.

When everything was ready, Koolee cracked the whip at the dogs. Tooky ran ahead to her place as leader, the other dogs began to pull, and the whole procession started back to the village, leaving a great red stain on the clean white snow where the bear had been killed.

Last of all came the twins and Koko. They had loaded the bear's skin on Menie's sled.

"It's a woman's work to pull the meat home. We men just do the hunting and fishing," Menie said to Koko. They had heard the men say that.

"Yes, we found the bear," Koko answered. "Monnie can pull the skin home."

And though Monnie had found the bear just as much as they had, she didn't say a word. She just pulled away on the sled, and they all reached the igloo together just as the round red sun came up out of the sea, and threw long blue shadows far across the fields of snow.

CHAPTER II. KOOLEE DIVIDES THE MEAT

I.

The first thing that was done after they got the sledge back to the village was to feed the dogs. The dogs were very hungry; they had smelled the fresh meat for a long time without so much as a bite of it, and they had had nothing to eat for two whole days. They jumped about and howled again and got their harnesses dreadfully tangled.

Kesshoo unharnessed them and gave them some bones, and while they were crunching them and quarreling among themselves, Koolee crawled into the igloo and brought out a bowl. The bowl was made of a hollowed-out stone, and it had water in it.

"This is for a charm," said Koolee. "If you each take a sip of water from this bowl my son will always have good luck in spying bears!"

She passed the bowl around, and each person took a sip of the water. When Menie's turn came he took a big, big mouthful, because he wanted to be very brave, indeed, and find a bear every week. But he was in too much of a hurry. The water went down his "Sunday-throat" and choked him! He coughed and strangled and his face grew red. Koolee thumped him on the back.

"That's a poor beginning for a great bear-hunter," she said.

Everybody laughed at Menie. Menie hated to be laughed at. He went away and found Nip and Tup. They wouldn't laugh at him, he knew. He thought he liked dogs better than people anyway.

Nip and Tup were trying to get their noses into the circle with the other dogs, but the big dogs snapped at them and drove them away, so Menie got some scraps and fed them.

Meanwhile Koolee stood by the sledge and divided the meat among her neighbors. First she gave one of the hind legs to the wives of the Angakok, because he always had to have the best of everything. She gave the kidneys to Koko's mother. To each one she gave just the part she had asked for. When each woman had been given her share, Kesshoo took what was left and put it on the storehouse.

The storehouse wasn't really a house at all. It was just a great stone platform standing up on legs, like a giant's table. The meat was placed on the top of it, so the dogs could not reach it, no matter how high they jumped.

II.

When the rest of the meat was taken care of, Koolee took the bear's head and carried it into the igloo.

All the people followed her. Then Koolee did a queer thing. She placed the head on a bench, with the nose pointing toward the Big Rock, because the bear had come from that direction. Then she stopped up the nostrils with moss and grease. She greased the bear's mouth, too.

"Bears like grease," she said. "And if I stop up his nose like that bears will never be able to smell anything. Then the hunters can get near and kill them before they know it." You see Koolee was a great believer in signs and in magic. All the other people were too.

She called to the twins, "Come here, Menie and Monnie."

The twins had come in with the others, but they were so short they were out of sight in the crowd. They crawled under the elbows of the grown people and stood beside Koolee.

"Look, children," she said to them, "your grandfather, who is dead, sent you this bear. He wants you to send him something. In five days the bear's spirit will go to the land where your grandfather's spirit lives. What would you like to have the bear's spirit take to your grandfather for a gift?"

"I'll send him the little fish that father carved for me out of bone," said Menie. He squirmed through the crowd and got it from a corner of his bed and brought it to his mother. She put it on the bear's head.

Monnie gave her a leather string with a lucky stone tied to it. Koolee put that on the bear's head too.

Then she said, "There! In five days' time the bear's spirit will give the shadows of these things to your grandfather. Then we can eat the head, but not until we are sure the bear's spirit has reached the home of the Dead."

"That is well," the Angakok said to the twins, when Koolee had finished. "Your grandfather will be pleased with your presents, I know. Your grandfather was a just man. I knew him well. He always paid great respect to me. Whenever he brought a bear home he gave me not only a hind leg, but the liver as well! I should not be surprised if he sent the bear this way, knowing how fond I am of bear's liver."

The Angakok placed his hand on his stomach and rolled up his eyes. "But times are not what they once were," he went on. "People care now only for their own stomachs! They would rather have the liver themselves than give it to the Angakok! They will be sorry when it is too late."

He shook his head and heaved a great sigh. Koolee looked at Kesshoo. She was very anxious. Kesshoo went out at once to the storehouse. He climbed to the top and got the liver.

By this time all the people had crawled out of the igloo again, and were ready to carry home their meat. Kesshoo ran to the Angakok and gave him the bear's liver. The Angakok handed it to one of his wives to carry. The other one already had the bear's leg. He said to Kesshoo, "You are a just man, like your father. I know the secrets of the sun, moon, and stars. You know your duty! You shall have your reward." He looked very solemn and waddled away toward his igloo with the two wives behind him carrying the meat. All the rest of the people followed after him and went into their own igloos.

CHAPTER III. THE TWINS GO FISHING

I.

When the people had all gone away, Menie and Monnie sat down on the side of the sledge. Nip and Tup were busy burying bones in the snow.
The other dogs had eaten all they wanted to and were now lying down asleep in the sun, with their noses on their paws.

Everything was still and cold. It was so still you could almost hear the silence, and so bright that the twins had to squint their eyes. In the air there was a faint smell of cooking meat.

Menie sniffed. "I'm so hungry I could eat my boots," he said.

"There are better things to eat than boots," Monnie answered. "What would you like best of everything in the world if you could have it?"

"A nice piece of blubber from a walrus or some reindeer tallow," said Menie.

"Oh, no," Monnie cried. "That isn't half as good as reindeer's stomach, or fishes' eyes! Um-m how I love fishes' eyes! I tell you, Menie, let's get something to eat and then go fishing, before the sun goes down!"

"All right," said Menie. "Let's see if Mother won't give us a piece of bear's fat! That is almost as good as blubber or fishes' eyes."

II.

They dived into the igloo. Their mother was standing beside the oil lamp, putting strands of dried moss into the oil. This lamp was their only stove and their only light. It didn't look much like our stoves. It was just a piece of soapstone, shaped something like a clamshell. It was hollowed out so it would hold the oil. All along the shallow side of the pan there were little tendrils of dried moss, like threads. These were the wicks.

Over the fire pan there was a rack, and from the rack a stone pan hung down over the lamp flame. It was tied by leather thongs to the rack. In the pan a piece of bear's meat was simmering. The fire was not big enough to cook it very well, but there was a little steam rising from it, and it made a very good smell for hungry noses.

"We're hungry enough to eat our boots," Menie said to his mother.

"You must never eat your boots; you have but one pair!" his mother answered. She pinched Menie's cheek and laughed at him.

Then she cut two chunks of fat from a piece of bear's meat which lay on the bench. She gave one to each of the twins. "Eat this, and soon you can have some cooked meat," she said. "It isn't quite done yet."

"We don't want to wait for the cooked meat," cried Monnie. "We want to go fishing before the sun is gone. Give us more fat and we'll eat it outside."

"You may go fishing if your father will go with you and cut holes for you in the ice," said her mother.

Koolee cut off two more pieces of fat. The twins took a piece in each hand. Then their mother reached down their own little fishing rods, which were stuck in the walls of the igloo. The twins had bear's meat in both hands. They didn't see how they could manage the fishing rods too.

But Menie thought of a way. "I'll show you how," he said to Monnie. He held one chunk of meat in his teeth! In his left hand he held the fishing rod, in his right he carried the other piece of meat!

Monnie did exactly what Menie did, and then they crawled down into the tunnel.

III.

The twins had some trouble getting out of the tunnel because both their hands were full. And besides the fishing rods kept getting between their legs. When they got outside they both took great bites of the bear's fat.

Kesshoo was hanging the dogs' harnesses up on a tall pole, where the dogs could not get them. The pole was eight feet long, and it was made of the tusk of a narwhal. The harnesses were made of walrus thongs and the dogs would eat them if they had a chance. That was the reason Kesshoo hung them out of reach. The twins ran to their father at once. They began to tell him that they wanted to go fishing right away before the sun went down but their mouths were so full they couldn't get the words out!

"Mm-m-m-m," Menie began, chewing with all his might!

Then Monnie did a shocking thing! She swallowed her meat whole, she was in such hurry! It made a great lump going down her throat! It almost choked her. But she shut her eyes, jerked her head forward, and got it down!

"Will you make two holes in the ice for us to fish through?" she said. She got the words out first! Then she took another bite of meat.

"Have you got your lines ready, and anything for bait?" asked their father.

By this time Menie had swallowed his mouthful too. He said, "We can take a piece of bear's meat for bait. The lines and hooks are ready."

Kesshoo looked at the lines. The rods were very short. They were made of driftwood with a piece of bone bound to the end by tough thongs.

There was a hole in the end of the bone, and through this hole the line was threaded. The line was made of braided reindeer thongs. On the end of the line was a hook carved out of bone.

"Your lines are all right," said Kesshoo. "Come along."

He led the way down to the beach. The twins came tumbling after him, and I am sorry to tell you they gobbled their meat all the way! After the twins came Nip and Tup. The ice was very thick. Kesshoo and the twins and the pups walked out on it quite a distance from the shore.

Kesshoo cut two round holes in the ice. One was for Menie and one for Monnie. The holes were not big enough for them to fall into.

By this time the twins had eaten all their meat except some small pieces which they saved for bait. They each put a piece of meat on the hook. Then they squatted down on their heels and dropped the hooks into the holes.

Kesshoo went back to the village, and left them there. "Don't stay out too long," he called back to them.

IV.

The twins sat perfectly still for a long time. Nip sat beside Menie, and Tup sat beside Monnie. It grew colder and colder. The sun began to drop down toward the sea again. At last it rested like a great round red wheel right on the Edge of the World!

Slowly, slowly it sank until only a little bit of the red rim showed; then that too was gone. Great splashes of red color came up in the sky over the place where it had been.

Still the twins sat patiently by their holes. It grew darker and darker. The colors faded. The stars began to twinkle, but the twins did not move. Nip and Tup ran races on the ice, and rolled over each other and barked.

At last, all of a sudden, there was a fearful jerk on Monnie's line! It took her by surprise. The little rod flew right out of her hands! Monnie flung herself on her stomach on the ice and caught the rod just as it was going down the hole! She held on hard and pulled like everything.

"I believe I've caught a whale," she panted.

But she never let go! She got herself right side up on the ice, somehow, and pulled and pulled on her line.

"Let me pull him in!" cried Menie. He tried to take her rod.

"Get away," screamed Monnie. "I'll pull in my own fish."

Menie danced up and down with excitement, still holding his own rod. The pups danced and barked too. Monnie never looked at any of them. She kept her eyes fixed on the hole and pulled.

At last she shrieked, "I've got him, I've got him!" And up through the hole came a great big codfish!

My! how he did flop around on the ice! Nip and Tup were scared. They ran for home at the first flop.

"Let's go home now," said Monnie. "I want to show my fine big fish to Mother."

But Menie said, "Wait a little longer till I catch one! I'll give you one eye out of my fish if you will."

Monnie waited. She put another piece of meat on her hook and dropped it again into the hole. After a while she said, "You can keep your old eye if you get it. It's so dark the fish can't see to get themselves caught anyway. I'm cold. I'm going home."

Menie got up very slowly and pulled up his line.

As they turned toward the shore, Monnie cried out, "Look, look! The sky is on fire!" It looked like it, truly!

Great white streamers were flashing from the Edge of the World, clear up into the sky! They danced like flames. Sometimes they shot long banners of blue or green fire up to the very stars. Overhead the sky shone red as blood. The stars seemed blotted out.

The twins had seen many wonderful things in the sky, but never such color as this. Their eyes grew as round and big and popping as those of Monnie's codfish, while they watched the long banners join themselves into a great waving curtain of color that hung clear across the heavens.

"What is it? Oh, what is it?" they gasped. They were too astonished to move, and they were a good deal frightened, too. They never knew the sky could act like that.

Monnie felt her black hair rise under her little fur hood. She seized Menie's coat. "Do you suppose the world is going to be burned up?" she said.

Just then they heard a voice calling, "Menie, Monnie, where are you?"

"Here we are," they answered. Their teeth were chattering with cold and fright, and they ran up the slope and flung themselves into their mother's arms.

"Oh, Mother, what is the matter with the sky?" they gasped.

Then Koolee looked up too. The long streamers were still flinging themselves up toward the red dome overhead.

We call this the "aurora," or "northern lights," and know that electricity causes it, but the twins' mother couldn't know that. She told them just what had been told her when she was a little girl.

She said, "That is the dance of the Spirits of the Dead! Haven't you ever seen it before?"

"Not like this," said the twins. "This is so big, and so red!"

"The sky is not often so bright," said Koolee. "Some say it is the spirits of little children dancing and playing together in the sky! They will not hurt you. You need not be afraid. See how they dance in a ring all around the Edge of the World! They look as if they were having fun."

"It goes around the Edge of the World just like the flames around our lamp," said Menie. "Maybe it's the Giants' lamp!"

Menie and Monnie believed in Giants. So did their mother. They thought the Giants lived in the middle of the Great White World, where the snow never melts.

The thought of the Giants scared them all. The twins gave the fish to their mother, and then they all three scuttled up the snowy slope toward the bright window of their igloo just as fast as they could go. When they got inside they found some hot bear's meat waiting for them, and Monnie had both the eyes from her fish to eat. But she gave one to Menie.

When they were warmed and fed, they pulled off their little fur suits, crawled into the piles of warm skins on the sleeping bench, and in two minutes were sound asleep.

CHAPTER IV. THE SNOW HOUSE

I.

It is very hard to tell what day it is, or what hour in the day, in a place where the days and nights are all mixed up, and where there are no clocks.

Menie and Monnie had never seen a clock in their whole lives. If they had they would have thought it was alive, and perhaps would have been afraid of it.

But people everywhere in the world get sleepy, so the Eskimos sometimes count their time by "sleeps." Instead of saying five days ago, they say "five sleeps" ago.

The night after the bear was killed it began to snow. The wind howled around the igloo and piled the snow over it in huge drifts.

The dogs were buried under it and had to be dug out, all but Nip and Tup. They stayed inside with the twins and slept in their bed.

The twins and their father and mother were glad to stay in the warm hut.

At last the snow stopped, the air cleared, and the twins and Kesshoo went out. Koolee stayed in the igloo.

She sat on her sleeping bench upon a pile of soft furs. A bear's skin was stretched up on the wall behind her. She had a cozy nest to work in.

The lamp stood on the bench beside her. She was making a beautiful new suit for Menie. It was made of fawn-skin as soft as velvet, and the hood and sleeves were trimmed with white rabbit's fur.

Her thimble was made of ivory, and her needle too. Her thread was a fine strip of hide. There was a bunch of such thread beside her.

Soon Kesshoo came in, bringing with him a dried fish and a piece of bear's meat, from the storehouse.

Koolee looked up from her sewing. "Isn't it five sleeps since you killed the bear?" she said.

Kesshoo counted on his fingers. "Yes," he said, "it is five sleeps."

"Then it is time to eat the bear's head," said Koolee. "His spirit is now with our fathers."

"Why not have a feast?" said Kesshoo. "There hasn't been any fresh meat in the village since the bear was killed, and I don't believe the rest have had anything to eat but dried fish. We have plenty of bear's meat still."

Koolee hopped down off the bench and put some more moss into the lamp.

"You bring in the meat," she said, "and tell the twins to go to all the igloos and invite the people to come at sunset."

"All right," Kesshoo answered, and he went out at once to the storehouse to get the meat.

II.

When he came out of the tunnel, Kesshoo found the twins trying to make a snow house for the dogs. They weren't getting on very well.

Kesshoo could make wonderful snow houses. He had made a beautiful one when the first heavy snows of winter had come, and the family had lived in it while Koolee finished building the stone igloo. The twins had watched him make it. It seemed so easy they were sure they could do it too. Kesshoo said, "If you will run to all the igloos and tell the people to come at sunset to eat the bear's head, I will help you build the snow house for the dogs."

Menie and Monnie couldn't run. Nobody could. The snow was too deep. They went in every step above their knees. But they ploughed along and gave their message at each igloo.

Everybody was very glad to come, and Koko said, "I'll come right now and stay if you want me to."

"Come along," said the twins.

They went back to their own house, kicking the snow to make a path. Koko went with them. The snow was just the right kind for a snow house. It packed well and made good blocks.

While the twins were away giving the invitations, Kesshoo carried great pieces of bear's meat into the house.

Koolee put in the cooking pan all the meat it would hold, and kept the blaze bright in the lamp underneath to cook it.

Then Kesshoo took his long ivory knife and went out to help the twins with the snow house, as he had promised.

"See, this is the way," he said to them.

He took an unbroken patch of snow where no one had stepped. He made a wide sweep of his arm and marked a circle in the snow with his knife.

The circle was just as big as he meant the house to be. Then he cut out blocks of snow from the space inside the circle. He placed these big blocks of snow around the circle on the line he had marked with his knife.

When he got the first row done Menie said, "I can do that! Let me try."

He took the knife and cut out a block. It wasn't nice and even like his father's blocks.

"That will never do," his father said. "Your house will tumble down unless your blocks are true."

He made the sides of the block straight by cutting off some of the snow.

"Now all the other blocks in this row must be just like this one," he said. Koko tried next. His block was almost right the first time. But then, as I have told you before, Koko was six.

Monnie tried the next one. I am sorry to say hers wouldn't do at all. It was dreadfully crooked. They took turns. Menie cut a new block while Koko placed the last one on the snow wall.

Kesshoo had to put on the top blocks to make the roof. Neither Koko nor Menie could do it right, though they tried and tried. It is a very hard thing to do. When the blocks were all laid up and the dome finished, Kesshoo said, "Now, Monnie can help pack it with snow."

Monnie got the snow shovel. The snow shovel was made of three flat pieces of wood sewed together with leather thongs. It had an edge of horn sewed on with thongs, too.

Monnie threw loose snow on the snow house and spatted it down with the back of the shovel.

While she was doing this, Menie and Koko built a tunnel entrance for the dogs just like the big one on the stone house.

They worked so hard they were warm as toast, though it was as cold as our coldest winter weather; and when it was all finished Menie ran clear over it just to show how strong and well built it was.

III.

When the snow house was all ready, Menie called the three big dogs. Tooky was the leader, and the three dogs together were Kesshoo's sledge team. Tooky was a hunting dog too.

When Menie called the dogs, the dogs thought they were going to be harnessed, so they hid behind the igloo and pretended they didn't hear. Koko and Menie followed them, but the moment they got near, the dogs bounded away. They went round to the front of the igloo and ran into the tunnel.

Koolee was just turning the meat in the pan with a pointed stick. There was a piece of bear's meat lying on the bench.

The dogs smelled the meat. They stuck their heads into the room, and when Koolee's back was turned, Tooky stole the meat!

Just then Koolee turned around. She saw Tooky. She shrieked, "Oh, my meat, my meat!" and whacked Tooky across the nose with the snow stick!

But Tooky was bound to have the meat. She ran out of the tunnel with it in her mouth, just as Menie and Koko got round to the front of the igloo once more.

"I-yi! I-yi!" they screamed, "Tooky's got the meat!" Kesshoo caught up his dog-whip and came running from the storehouse.

The other two dogs wanted the meat too. They flew at Tooky and snarled and fought with her to get it.

Then Koolee's head appeared in the tunnel hole! Tooky was crouching in the snow in front of the tunnel, trying to fight off the other two dogs and guard the meat at the same time.

She wasn't doing a thing with her tail, but she was very busy with all the rest of her. Her tail was pointed right toward the tunnel.

The moment she saw it Koolee seized the tail with both hands and jerked it like everything! Tooky was so surprised she yelped. And when she opened her mouth to yelp, of course she dropped the meat.

Just at that instant Kesshoo's whip lash came singing about the ears of all three dogs.

"Snap, snap," it went. They jumped to get out of the way of the lash.

Then Koolee leaped forward and snatched the meat from under their noses, and scuttled back with it into the tunnel before you could say Jack Robinson.

It is dangerous to snatch meat away from hungry dogs. If Kesshoo hadn't been slashing at them with his whip, and if Menie and Koko hadn't been screaming at them with all their might, so the dogs were nearly distracted, Koolee might have been badly bitten.

Just then Monnie came up with some dried fish. She threw one of the fish over in front of the snow house.

The dogs saw it and leaped for it. Then she threw another into the snow hut itself. They went after that. She fed them all with dried fish until they were so full they curled up in the snow house and went to sleep.

CHAPTER V. THE FEAST

I

The moment the sun had gone out of sight all the people in the village came pouring out of their tunnels on their way to the feast at Kesshoo's house.

Kesshoo's house was so small that it seemed as if all the people could not possibly get into it.

But the Eskimos are used to crowding into very small spaces, indeed. Sometimes a man and his wife and all his children will live in a space about the size of a big double bed.

First the Angakok came out of his igloo, looking fatter than ever. The Angakok always found plenty to eat somehow. Both his wives were thin. Their faces looked like baked apples all brown and wrinkled.

When they reached Kesshoo's house, the Angakok went into the tunnel first.

Now I can't tell you whether he had grown fatter during the five days, or whether the entrance had grown smaller, but this much I know: the Angakok got stuck! He couldn't get himself into the room no matter how much he tried! He squirmed and wriggled and twisted, until his face was very red and he looked as if he would burst, but there he stayed.

Other people had crawled into the tunnel after him. His two wives were just behind. Everybody got stuck, of course, because no one could move until the Angakok did. He was just like a cork in the neck of a bottle.

Kesshoo and Koolee and the twins and Nip and Tup were all in the igloo. When they saw the Angakok's face come through the hole they thought, of course, the rest of him would come too. But it didn't, and the Angakok was mad about it.

"Why don't they build igloos the way they used to?" he growled. "Every year the tunnels get smaller and smaller! Am I to remain here forever?" he went on. "Why doesn't somebody help me?"

Kesshoo and Koolee seized him under his arms. They pulled and pulled. The two wives pushed him from behind.

"I-yi! I-yi!" screamed the Angakok. "You will scrape my skin off!"

He kicked out behind with his feet. His wives backed hastily, to get out of the way. That made them bump into Koko's mother who was just behind them. Her baby was in her hood, and when she backed, the baby's head was bumped on the roof of the tunnel.

The baby began to roar. In the tunnel it sounded like a clap of thunder. The wives of the Angakok and Koko's mother all began to talk at once, and with that and the baby's crying I suppose there never was a tunnel that held so much noise. It all came into the igloo, and it sounded quite frightful. The twins crept into the farthest corner of the sleeping bench and watched their father and mother and the Angakok, with their eyes almost popping out of their heads.

Nip and Tup thought they would help a little, so they jumped off the bench; and barked at the Angakok. You see, they didn't know he was a great medicine man. They thought maybe he ought not to be there at all.

Nip even snapped at the Angakok's ear!

That made the Angakok more angry than ever. He reached into the room, seized Nip with one hand and flung him up on to the sleeping bench. Nip lit on top of Menie. Nip was very much surprised, and so was Menie.

Now, whether the jerk he gave in throwing Nip did it or not, I cannot say, but at that instant Kesshoo and Koolee both gave a great pull in front. At the same moment the two wives gave a great push behind, and the next moment after that, there was the Angakok, still red, and still angry, sitting on the edge of the sleeping bench in the best place near the fire!

Then his two wives came crawling through. The Angakok looked at them as if he thought they had made him stick in the tunnel, and had done it on purpose, too. The wives scuttled up on to the sleeping bench, and got into the farthest corner of it as fast as they could.

The women and children always sat back on the bench at a feast.

When Koko's mother came in, the baby was still crying. She climbed up on to the bed with him, and Menie and Monnie showed him the pups and that made the baby laugh again.

As fast as they came in, the women and children packed themselves away on the sleeping bench. The men sat along the edge of it with their feet on the floor.

II.

The smell of food soon made everybody cheerful. When at last they were all crowded into the room, Koolee placed the bear's head and other pans of meat on the floor.

Then she crawled back on to the bench with the other women.

The Angakok was the first one to help himself. He reached down and took a large chunk of meat. He held it up to his mouth and took hold of the end with his teeth. Then he sawed off a huge mouthful with his knife.

It looked as if he would surely cut off the end of his nose too, but he didn't.

When the men had all helped themselves, pieces of meat were handed out to the women and children.

Soon they were all eating as if their lives depended on it. And now I think of it, their lives did depend on it, to be sure! I will not speak about their table manners. In fact, they hadn't any to speak of! They had nothing to eat with the meat, not even salt, but it was a great feast to them for all that, and they ate and ate until every scrap was gone.

The Angakok grew better natured every minute. By the time he had eaten all he could hold he was really quite happy and benevolent! He clasped his hands over his stomach and smiled on everybody.

The women chattered in their corner of the sleeping-bench, and Koolee showed Koko's mother the new fur suit trimmed with white rabbit's skin that she was making for Menie. And Koko's mother said she really must make one for Koko just like it.

The twins and Koko talked about a trap to catch hares which they meant to made as soon as the long days began again, and the baby went to sleep on a pile of furs in the corner. Menie fed the pups with some of his own meat, and gave them each a bone. Nip and Tup buried their bones under the baby and then went to sleep too.

III.

After a while the Angakok turned his face to the wall, as he always did when he meant to tell a story or sing a song. Then he said, "Listen, my children!" He called everybody, even the grown up people, his children! Everybody listened. They always listened when the Angakok spoke.

The Angakok knew the secrets of the sun, moon, and stars. He had told them so many times! The people believed it, and it may be that the Angakok really believed it himself, though I have some doubt about that.

"Listen, my children," said the Angakok, "and I will tell you wonderful things.

"There is a world beneath the sea! You catch glimpses of that world yourselves in calm summer weather, when the water is still, and you know that I speak the truth!

"Then you can see the shadows of rocks and islands and glaciers in the smooth water. Far below you see blue sky and white clouds. That is the calm world in which the Spirits of the Dead live. I have visited that underworld, many times, I have talked there with the spirits of your ancestors."

The Angakok paused and looked around to see if every one was paying attention. Then he went on with his story.

"Do you remember how two springs ago there were so few walruses and seals along the coast that you nearly died for lack of food and oil?" he said. "My children, it was I who brought the seals and walruses back to you! Without my efforts you might all have starved!

"I will tell you of the perils of a fearful journey which I undertook for your sakes. Then you will see what you owe to the skill and faithfulness of your Angakok!"

All the people looked very solemn, and nodded their heads. The Angakok went on.

"You must know that in the depths of the underworld, far beyond the beautiful abode of the Spirits of the Dead, lives the Old Woman of the Sea!

"There she sits forever and forever beside a monstrous lamp. Underneath the lamp is a great saucer to catch the oil which drips from it.

"In that saucer there are whole flocks of sea-birds swimming about! All the animals that live in the sea, the whales and walruses, the codfish and the seals, swarm in the saucer of the Old Woman of the Sea. That is where they all come from. Sometimes the Old Woman of the Sea keeps all the creatures in the saucer. Then there are no seal or fish or walrus along our coasts, and there is hunger among the innuit (human beings).

"At the time of my journey she had kept all the creatures for so long a time in her saucer that you and many others were nearly dead for lack of food."

"It was then that I prepared myself for the perils of this journey to the underworld. I called my Tornak, or guiding spirit, to lead my steps. Without his Tornak an Angakok can do nothing. The Tornak came at once in answer to my call. He took me by the hand, and we plunged down into the water. First we passed through the beautiful World of Spirits, where it is always summer. This part of the way was quite pleasant, but on the farther side of that world we came to a fearful abyss. It could be crossed only on a large slippery wheel, as slippery as ice."

"I mounted this wheel and was whirled across the chasm. No sooner had I reached the other side than new terrors came upon me. I had to pass by great cauldrons of boiling oil, in which seals were swimming about."

"A misstep would have sent me plunging into the boiling oil, and you would have lost your Angakok forever!"

The thought of this was so dreadful that the Angakok paused and wiped his eyes. Then he went on again with his story.

"However, with great courage I kept upon my way until at last I saw the Old Woman's house! A deep gulf lay between us and her dwelling, and outside it stood a great dog with bloody jaws. This dog guards the entrance, and he sleeps only for a single moment, once in a very great while."

"For six days I and my Tornak waited there for the dog to sleep. At last on the seventh day he closed his eyes! Instantly the Tornak seized my hand and drew me across the bridge which spanned the chasm. This bridge was as narrow as a single thread."

"When we were safely across the bridge we passed the sleeping dog and boldly entered the Old Woman's house. The Old Woman is terrible to look upon! Her hand is the size of a large walrus, and her teeth like the rocks along the coast!" The Angakok dropped his voice to a whisper.

"However, when she looked upon me she trembled!" he said. "She saw at once that I possessed great power, and was a great Angakok. I spoke to her flattering words. Then I told her of the hunger of my children!"

"I begged that she would send the seal and walrus and sea-birds to our coast at once. But she had no mind to yield to my requests. Then I stormed and threatened." The Angakok's voice grew louder. "The walls shook with the thunder of my voice! At last I seized her by the hair! I tipped over the saucer with my foot! My great power prevailed against the mighty sorceress!"

"The seal and walrus swam away. The birds flew into the air and were gone. I had conquered the Old Woman of the Sea! My children were saved!" The Angakok was silent for a moment. Then he spoke again in a natural voice.

"When I opened my eyes in my own igloo again," he said, "the famine was already over. Flocks of sea-birds were flying overhead. The sea swarmed with fish, and with walrus and seal. Every one along the whole coast was happy. Ask yourselves, is it not so?"

The Angakok seemed very much pleased with himself, and he looked about, as if he expected every one else to be pleased with him too. All the people were filled with wonder at his great power. They began to talk among themselves.

"Yes, I remember the famine well," said Koko's father. "I was away up the coast that season. Several died in our village for lack of food."

Other men remembered things about other times when food had been scarce.

"It is lucky," they said to each other, "that here we have a great Angakok who understands all the secrets of the World and who can save us from such dreadful things."

IV.

At last Kesshoo said, "Will you tell us, great Angakok, how you make these wonderful journeys?"

"Do you really wish to know?" asked the Angakok. "If you do, I will summon my guiding spirits to tell you, but they will speak only in the darkness."

Kesshoo took the lamp at once and put it out in the tunnel. Then he placed a thick musk-ox hide over the entrance, so that not a single ray of light came into the room. The darkness could almost be felt. Everybody sat very still and listened.

Soon a heavy body was heard to strike the floor with a dull thud, and a strange voice said, "Who calls me?"

Another voice said, "You are called, mighty spirits, to tell these children of the labors of their Angakok."

Then began all sorts of strange noises, as of different persons speaking. All the voices sounded much like the Angakok's, and they all said what a great medicine man the Angakok was, and how every one in the village must be sure to do what he told them to!

At last the Angakok himself spoke, in his own voice. "I will tell you how I make these strange journeys," he said.

"My body is now lying on the floor at your feet. Now I begin to rise. You cannot see me. You cannot touch me. Now I am floating about your heads, now I am touching the roof! I can go wherever I please! Nothing can stop me! I know the secret places of the sun, moon, and stars. I can fly through the roof and go at once to the moon, if I wish to."

Then the voice was still. Nobody moved or spoke.

Monnie had gone to sleep in the corner of the bed, but Koko and Menie were still awake. They had listened to every word about the Old Woman of the Sea, and how the Angakok traveled to the moon.

You know I told you before that Koko was six. He wanted to know all about things. So he spoke right out in the dark, when every one else was still.

He said, "Mother, if the Angakok can go anywhere he wants to, why couldn't he get out of the tunnel?"

Koko's mother tried to hush him up. "Sh, sh," she said, and put her hand over his mouth. At least she thought she did, but she made a mistake in the dark and put her hand over Menie's mouth instead!

Menie tried to say, "I never said a word," but he could only make queer sounds, because Koko's mother's hand was tight on his mouth.

Of course Koko didn't know his mother was trying to keep him still, so he said again, "Why is it, mother?"

Koko's mother heard Koko's voice speaking just as plainly as ever though she was sure she had her hand over his mouth! She was frightened.

"Magic! magic!" she screamed. "Bring the light! Koko is bewitched! I have my hand over his mouth, yet you hear that he talks as plainly as ever!"

Koko tried to say, "Your hand isn't over my mouth," and Menie tried to say, "It's over mine!" but he could only say, "M-m-m," because she held on so tight!

Koko's mother was making so much noise herself that she wouldn't have heard what either one said anyway. The baby woke up and whimpered. Nip and Tup woke up and barked like everything.

Kesshoo got the light from the tunnel as quickly as he could, and set it on the bench. Then every one saw what was the matter! They all laughed, all but Menie and the Angakok. The Angakok said to Koko's father, "You'd better look after that boy. He is disrespectful to me. That is a bad beginning!"

Koko's father was ashamed of him. He said, "Koko is so small!"

But the Angakok said, "Koko is six. He is old enough to know better."

V.

Everybody was so glad to see the light again that they all began to talk at once.

Some one said to Kesshoo, "Tell us about the long journey to the south you took once long ago."

Then everybody else listened, while Kesshoo told about how once he had taken his dog sledge with a load of musk-ox and seal skins on it far down the coast and how at last he had come to a little settlement where the houses were all made of wood, if they would believe it!

He told them that in the bay before the village there was a boat as big as the Big Rock itself. It had queer white wings, and the wind blew on these wings and made the boat go!

Kesshoo had been out in a kyak to see it. He had even paddled all round it. The men on the great boat had fair hair, and one of them, the chief man of all, had bought some of Kesshoo's skins and one of his dogs. The man was a great chief. His name was Nansen.

This great chief had told Kesshoo that he was going to take a sledge and go straight into the inland country where the Giants live! He said he was going to cross the great ice! No man had ever done that since the world began.

Kesshoo thought probably the great chief had been eaten by the Giants, but he did not know surely, because he had never been back there since to find out. And to be sure, if he had been eaten by Giants, no one ever would know about it anyway.

Then Kesshoo showed them all a great knife that the white chief had given him, in exchange for a sealskin, and two steel needles that he had sent to Koolee. Koolee kept the needles in a little ivory case all by themselves.

She always carried the case in her kamik, so it would not be lost. She could do wonderful sewing with the needles. Koolee was very proud of her sewing. No one else in the whole village could sew so well, because they had not such good needles to do it with. Koolee used them only for her very finest work.

At last the Angakok said, "It is time to go home." He called to his wives. They climbed down off the bench.

That started the others. One after another they put on their upper garments, which they had taken off in the warm igloo, said good bye, and popped down into the tunnel. Last of all came the Angakok's turn.

Then Kesshoo and Koolee and the Angakok's wives all began to look very anxious. The Angakok looked a little worried himself. If he had stuck coming in, what would happen now after he had eaten so much!

He got down on his hands and knees, and looked at the hole. He had taken off his thick fur coat when he came in. Now he took off his undercoat, and his thick fur trousers! He gave them to his wives.

Then he stretched himself out just as long as he possibly could and slowly hitched himself down into the tunnel, groaning all the way.

Kesshoo and Koolee and the wives waited until his feet disappeared, and they heard him scraping along through the tunnel. Then they breathed a great sigh of relief, and the two wives popped down after him.

The last Kesshoo and Koolee heard of the Angakok, was a kind of muffled roar when a piece of ice fell from the top of the tunnel on to his bare back.

Menie and Monnie and the pups were already sound asleep in their corner of the bench when their father and mother fixed the lamp for the night and crawled in among the fur robes beside them.

CHAPTER VI. THE REINDEER HUNT

I.

The day after the feast it was still very cold, but there were signs of spring in the air. When Menie went out to feed the dogs, he saw a flock of ravens flying north, and Koko saw some sea-birds on the same day.

Two days after that, when the twins and Koko were all three playing together on the Big Rock, they saw a huge iceberg float lazily by.

It had broken away from a glacier, farther north, and was drifting slowly toward the Southern Sea. It gleamed in the sun like a great ice palace.

One morning the air was thick with fog. When Kesshoo saw the fog he said, "This would be a great day to hunt reindeer."

"Oh, let me go with you!" cried Menie.

Monnie knew better than to ask. She knew very well she would never be allowed to go.

Kesshoo thought a little before he answered. Then he said, "If Koko's father will go, too, you and Koko may both go with us. You are pretty small to go hunting, but boys cannot begin too early to learn."

Menie was wild with joy. He rushed to Koko's house and told him and his father what Kesshoo had said.

When he had finished, Koko's father said at once, "Tell Kesshoo we will go."

It was not long before they were ready to start. Kesshoo had his great bow, and arrows, and a spear. He also had his bird dart. Koko's father had his bow and spear and dart, too. Menie had his little bow and arrows.

Kesshoo put a harness on Tooky and tied the end of Tooky's harness trace around Menie's waist. Koko's father had brought his best dog, too, and Koko was fastened to the end of that dog's harness in the same way.

Then the four hunters started on their journey. Menie and Koko driving the dogs in front of them.

Monnie stood on the Big Rock and watched them until they were out of sight in the fog. Nip and Tup were with her. They wanted to go as much as Monnie did and she had hard work to keep them from following after the hunters.

II.

Kesshoo knew very well where to look for the reindeer. He led the way up a steep gorge where the first green moss appeared in the spring. They all four walked quietly along for several miles.

When they got nearly to the head of the gorge, Kesshoo stopped. He said to the boys, "You must not make any noise yourselves, and you must not let the dogs bark. If you do there will be no reindeer today."

The boys kept very still, indeed. The dogs were good hunting dogs. They knew better than to bark.

They walked on a little farther. Then Kesshoo came very near the others and spoke in a low voice. He said, "We are coming to a spot where there are likely to be reindeer. The wind is from the south. If we keep on in this direction, the reindeer will smell us. We must go round in such a way that the wind will carry the scent from them to us, not from us to them."

They turned to the right and went round to the north. They had gone only a short distance in this direction, when they found fresh reindeer tracks in the snow. The dogs began to sniff and strain at their harnesses.

"They smell the game," whispered Kesshoo. "Hold on tight! Don't let them run."

Menie and Koko held the dogs back as hard as they could. Kesshoo and Koko's father crept forward with their bows in their hands. The fog was so thick they could not see very far before them.

They had gone only a short distance, when out of the fog loomed two great gray shadows. Instantly the two men dropped on their knees and took careful aim.

The reindeer did not see them. They did not know that anything was near until they felt the sting of the hunters' arrows. One reindeer dropped to the earth. The other was not killed. He flung his head in the air and galloped away, and they could hear the thud, thud, of his hoofs long after he had disappeared in the fog.

The moment the dogs heard the singing sound of the arrows, they bounded forward. Koko and Menie were not strong enough to hold them back, and they could not run fast enough to keep up with them. So they just bumped along behind the dogs! Some of the time they slid through the snow.

The snow was rough and hard, and it hurt a good deal to be dragged through it as if they were sledges, but Eskimo boys are used to bumps, and they knew if they cried they might scare the game, so they never even whimpered.

It was lucky for them that they had not far to go. When they came bumping along, Kesshoo and Koko's father laughed at them.

"Don't be in such a hurry," they called. "There's plenty of time!"

They unbound the traces from Menie and Koko and hitched the dogs to the body of the reindeer. Then they all started back to the village with Koko's father driving the dogs.

Soon the fog lifted and the sky grew clear.

Monnie was playing with her doll in the igloo, when she heard Tooky bark. She knew it was Tooky at once. She and Koolee both plunged into the tunnel like mice down a mouse hole. Nip and Tup were ahead of them.

Outside they found Koko's mother and the baby. Koolee called to her, and she called to the wives of the Angakok, who were scraping a bear's skin in the snow.

The Angakok's wives, and Koko's mother and her baby, and Koolee, and Monnie, and Nip and Tup all ran to meet the hunters, and you never saw two prouder boys than Koko and Menie when they showed the reindeer to their mothers.

The mothers were proud of their young hunters, too. Koolee said, "Soon we shall have another man in our family."

When they were quite near the village again, they met the Angakok. He had been trying to catch up with them and he was out of breath from running. He looked at them sternly.

"Why didn't you call me?" he panted.

His wives looked frightened and didn't say a word. Nobody else said anything. The Angakok glared at them all for a moment. Then he poked the reindeer with his fingers to see if it was fat and said to the men, "Which portion am I to have?"

"Would you like the liver?" asked Kesshoo. He remembered about the bear's liver, you see.

But the Angakok looked offended. "Who will have the stomach?" he said. "You know very well that the stomach is the best part of a reindeer."

"Take the stomach, by all means, then," said Kesshoo, politely.

Koolee and Monnie looked very much disappointed. They wanted the stomach dreadfully.

But the Angakok answered, "Since you urge me, I will take the stomach. I had a dream last night, and in the dream I was told by my Tornak that today I should feed upon a reindeer's stomach, given me by one of my grateful children. When you think how I suffered to bring food to you, I am sure you will wish to provide me with whatever it seems best that I should have."

He stood by while Kesshoo and Koko's father skinned the reindeer and cut it in pieces. Then he took the stomach and disappeared into his igloo with his face all wreathed in smiles.

CHAPTER VII. WHAT HAPPENED WHEN MENIE AND KOKO WENT HUNTING BY THEMSELVES

I.

It was very lucky for the twins that their father was such a brave and skillful kyak man. You will see the reason why, when I tell you the story of the day Menie and Koko went hunting alone on the ice.

One April morning Kesshoo was working on his kyak to make sure that it was in perfect order for the spring walrus hunting. Koko and Menie watched him for a long time. Monnie was with Koolee in the hut.

By and by Koko said to Menie, "Let's go out on the ice and hunt for seal-holes."

"All right," said Menie. "You take your bow and arrows and I'll take my spear. Maybe we shall see some little auks."

Koko had a little bow made of deer's horns, and some bone arrows, and Menie had a small spear which his father had made for him out of driftwood.

"I'll tell you!" said Menie. "Let's go hunting just the way father does! You do the shooting and I'll do the spearing! Won't everybody be surprised to see us bring home a great load of game? I shall give everything I get to my mother."

"I'm going to hunt birds and seal-holes too," Koko answered.

Kesshoo was very busy fixing the fastening of his harpoon, and he did not hear what they said.

The two boys went to their homes for their weapons, and then ran out on the ice. Nobody knew where they were. Of course, Nip and Tup went along.

II.

All the way over the ice they looked for seal-holes. It takes sharp eyes to find them, for seal-holes are very small.

You see, the mother seals try to find the safest place they can to hide their babies, and this is the way they do it:

As soon as the ice begins to freeze in the autumn, the seals gnaw holes in it to reach the air, and they keep these holes open all winter. It freezes so fast in that cold country that they have to be busy almost every minute all through the winter breaking away the ice there. They get their sleep in snatches of a minute or so at a time, and between their naps they clear the ice from their breathing holes.

There is usually a deep layer of snow over the ice. Each mother seal hollows out a little igloo under the snow, around her breathing hole, and leaves a tiny hole in the top of it, so her baby can have plenty of fresh air and be hidden from sight at the same time.

The mother seal leaves the baby in the snow house, and she herself dives through the hole and swims away. Every few minutes she comes back to breathe, and to see that her baby is safe.

It was the tiny hole in the top of the seal's snow house that Menie and Koko hoped to find.

The days had grown quite long by this time and there was fog in the air. Once in a while there would be a loud crackling noise.

"The ice is beginning to break," Koko said. "Don't you hear it pop? My father says he thinks the warm weather will begin early this year."

They had gone some distance out on the ice, when suddenly Menie said, "Look! Look there!" He pointed toward the north. There not far from shore was a flock of sea-birds, resting on the ice.

"Just let me get a shot at them!" cried Koko. "You stay here and hold on to the dogs! Nip and Tup haven't any sense at all about game! They'll only scare them."

III.

Koko ran swiftly and quietly towards the birds. Menie sat on the ice and watched him and held Nip and Tup, one under each arm. When Koko got quite near the birds, he took careful aim and let fly an arrow at them.

It didn't hit any of the birds, but it frightened them. They flew up into the air and away to the north and alighted farther on. Koko followed them.

All at once Menie heard a queer little sound. It went "Plop-plop-plop," and it sounded very near. Nip and Tup sniffed, and began to growl and nose around on the ice.

Menie knew what the queer noise meant, for his father had told him all about seal hunting. It meant that a seal-hole was near, and that a seal had come up to breathe. It was the seal that made the "plopping" noise.

Menie tried to keep the dogs still, but they wouldn't be kept still. They ran round with their noses on the snow, giving little anxious whines, and short, sharp barks.

The "plop-plop" stopped. The seal had gone down under the ice, but Menie meant to find the hole. He went out quite near the open water in his search. At last, just beyond a hummock of ice, he saw it! He crept carefully up to it.

He lay down on his stomach and peeped into the hole to see what it was like. He could not see a thing!

Then he stuck his lance down. His lance touched something soft that wiggled! Menie stood up. He was so excited that he trembled. He knew he had found a seal-hole with a live seal in the snow house!

With all his strength he struck his lance down through the snow. The snow house fell in and Menie fell with it, but he kept hold of his lance. The end of the lance was buried in the snow, but it was moving. Menie knew by this that he had stuck it into the seal!

He lay still and kept fast hold of his lance, and pressed down on it with all his might.

Nip and Tup were crazy with excitement. They jumped round and barked and tried to dig a hole in the snow with their forefeet.

At last the spear stopped wiggling. Then Menie carefully dug the snow away. There lay a little white seal! It was too young to swim away with its mother. That was why such a small boy as Menie had been able to kill it.

He dragged it out on the ice. He was so excited and so busy he did not notice how near he was to the open water.

IV.

All of a sudden there was a loud cracking noise, and Menie felt the ice moving under him! He looked back. There was a tiny strip of blue water between him and the shore!

The strip grew wider while he looked at it! Menie knew that he was adrift on an ice raft, and he was terribly frightened. Nip and Tup cuddled close to him and whined with fear.

Menie understood perfectly well that he might be carried far out to sea and never come back any more. He put his hands to his mouth and yelled with all his might!

Koko was still following the birds, and did not hear Menie's cries. Menie could see him running up the beach after the birds, and he could see his father working over his kyak near his home.

He even saw Monnie come out of the tunnel and go to watch her father at his work. They seemed very far away, and every moment the distance between them and the raft grew greater.

Menie screamed again and again. At the third scream he saw his father straighten up, shade his eyes with his hand, and look out to sea.

"Oh," Menie thought. "What if he shouldn't see me!" He shouted louder than ever! He waved his arms! He even pinched the tails of Nip and Tup and made them bark. Then he saw his father wave his hand and dive into the tunnel.

In another instant he was out again and pulling on his skin coat. Then he took the kyak on his shoulders and ran with it to the beach. Monnie and Koolee came running after him.

They were doing the screaming now! Every one in the village heard the screams and came running down to the beach, too.

When Menie saw his father coming with the kyak, he wasn't afraid any more, for he was sure his father would save him. He wasn't even afraid about the cakes of ice that were floating in the water, though there is nothing more dangerous than to go out in a kyak among ice floes. One bump from a floating cake of ice is enough to upset any boat, and I don't like to think of what might happen if a kyak should get between two big cakes of ice.

Kesshoo ran with his kyak as far as he could on the ice. Then he got in and fitted the bottom of his skin jacket over the kyak hole and carefully slid himself into the open water.

Once in the water, how his paddle flew!

It seemed to Menie as if his father would never reach him! He sat very still on the ice pan with the dead seal beside him, and Nip and Tup huddled up against him.

At last Kesshoo came near enough so he could make Menie hear everything he said. "Menie," he cried, "if you do exactly what I tell you to, I can save you.

"I will throw you my harpoon. You must drive it way down into the ice. Then by the harpoon line I will tow your ice pan back toward shore. When we get to the big ice I will find a place for you to land.

"You must be ready, and when I give the word jump from your ice raft on to the solid ice."

Then Kesshoo threw his harpoon, and Menie drove it into the ice with all his might. Slowly Kesshoo drew the line taut, turned his kyak round, and started for the shore. The journey out had been dangerous, but the journey back was much more so, for Kesshoo could not dodge the floating ice nearly so well. He had to pick his way carefully through the clearest water he could find. Very cautiously they moved toward shore.

V.

They were getting quite near the place where the ice had broken with Menie, when suddenly, right near them, they saw the head and great, round eyes of a seal! It was the seal mother.

She had come back to find her breathing hole and her baby.

The moment Kesshoo saw her he seized his dart, which lay in its place on top of his kyak, and threw it with all his might at the seal.

The seal dived down into the sea, but a bladder full of air was attached to the line on the dart, and this bladder floated on the water, so Kesshoo could tell by watching it just where the seal was.

Kesshoo knew he had struck the seal, and although he was already towing the ice raft, he was determined to bring home the big seal, too!

He called to Menie. "Sit still and wait until I come for you."

Then he quickly cut the harpoon line by which he was towing the ice raft, and set it adrift again. As soon as he was free he paddled away after the bladder, which was now bobbing along over the water at some little distance from the boat.

Menie sat perfectly still and watched his father. Kesshoo reached the bladder and began to pull on the line, but just at that moment the big seal turned round and swam right under the kyak!

In a second the kyak turned bottom side up in the water! Menie screamed. The people watching on the shore gave a great howl, and Koko's father started up the beach after his own kyak.

He thought perhaps Kesshoo could not manage both the ice raft and the seal, and he meant to go to help him.

But in one second Kesshoo was right side up again. No water could get into the kyak because Kesshoo's skin coat was drawn tight over the hole in the deck, and Kesshoo was in the coat!

Kesshoo often turned somersaults in the water in that way. Sometimes he even did it for fun! He said afterward that he could have turned the boat right side up again with just his nose, without using either his paddle or his arms, if only his nose had been a little bigger, and though he meant this for a joke, the twins believed that he really could do it.

The moment he was right side up again, Kesshoo gave chase once more to the bladder. The seal was very weak now, and Kesshoo knew that it would soon come to the surface and float and that then he could tow it in.

He had not long to wait. The bladder bobbed about for a while and then was still. Kesshoo drew up the line, and paddled back to the ice raft, towing the big seal after him.

"Catch this," he said to Menie. He threw him the end of the line. "Wind the line six times round the harpoon," he said, "and hold tight to the end of it."

Menie did as he was told. Then Kesshoo tied together the two ends of the harpoon line, which he had cut, and began to tow the ice raft back to share again.

Menie kept tight hold of the other line and towed the seal!

Kesshoo paddled slowly and carefully along, until at last there was only a little strip of water between the kyak and the solid ice.

But how in the world could Menie get across that strip of water to safety?

The kyak was between him and the solid ice, and Menie could not possibly get into the kyak. Neither could he swim. But Kesshoo knew a way.

He came up closer to the solid ice. Then he gave a great sweep with his paddle and lifted his kyak right up on to it. He sprang out, and, seizing the harpoon line, pulled Menie's raft close up to the edge of the firm ice.

Menie was still holding tight to the line that held the big seal.

Kesshoo threw him another line. Menie caught the end of it.

"Now tie the big seal's line fast to that," Kesshoo said. Menie was a very small boy, but he knew how to tie knots. He did just what his father told him to.

"Now," said his father, "pull up the harpoon." Menie did so. "Tie the harpoon line to the little seal." Menie did that. "Now throw the harpoon to me," commanded Kesshoo.

Menie threw it with all his might. His father caught it, and stood on the firm ice, holding in his hands the line that the big seal was tied to, and the harpoon, with its line fastened to the little seal.

"Now hold on to the little seal, and I will pull you right up against the solid ice, and when I say 'Jump,' you jump," said Kesshoo.

Slowly and very, carefully he pulled, until the raft grated against the solid ice.

"Jump!" shouted Kesshoo.

Menie jumped. The ice raft gave a lurch that nearly sent him into the water, but Kesshoo caught him and pulled him to safety.

A great shout of joy went up from the shore, and Menie was glad enough to shout too when he felt solid ice under his feet once more!

While he helped his father pull in the little seal, all the people came running out on to the ice to meet them, but Kesshoo sent back every one except Koko's father. He was afraid the ice might break again with so many people on it. Koko's father helped pull the big seal out of the water and over the ice to the beach.

Menie dragged his own little seal after him by the harpoon line, and when he came near the beach, the people all cried out, "See the great hunter with his game!" And Koolee was so glad to see Menie and so proud of her boy that she nearly burst with joy!

"I knew the charm would work," she cried. "Not only does he spy bears, he kills seals! And he only five years old!"

She put her arms around him and pressed her flat nose to his. That's the Eskimo way of kissing.

Menie tried to look as if he killed seals and got carried away on an ice pan every day in the week, but inside he felt very proud, too.

When Kesshoo and Koko's father came up with the big seal, Koolee and the other women dragged it to the village, where it was skinned and cut up. Every one had a piece of raw blubber to eat at once, and the very first piece went to Menie.

While they were eating it, Koko came back. He had gone so far up the shore hunting little auks that he hadn't seen a thing that had happened. And he hadn't killed any little auks either.

Koko felt that things were very unequally divided in this world. He wanted to kill a seal and get lost on a raft and be a hero too.

But Koolee gave him a large piece of blubber, and that made him feel much more cheerful again. He just said to Monnie, "If I had been with Menie, this never would have happened! I should not have let him get so near the edge of the ice! But then, you know, I am six, and he is only five, so, of course, he didn't know any better."

Everybody in the village had seal meat that night, and the Angakok had the head, which they all thought was the best part. He said he didn't feel very well, and his Tornak had told him nothing would cure him so quickly as a seal's head. So Koolee gave it to him.

The skin of the little white seal Koolee saved and dressed very carefully. She chewed it, all over, on the wrong side, and sucked out all the blubber, and made it soft and fine as velvet; and when that was done, she made out of it two beautiful pairs of white mittens for the twins.

CHAPTER VIII. THE WOMAN-BOATS

I.

During the long, dark hours of the winter Kesshoo found many pleasant things to do at home. He was always busy. He carved a doll for Monnie out of the ivory tusk of a walrus.

Monnie named the doll Annadore, and she loved it dearly. Koolee dressed Annadore in fur, with tiny kamiks of sealskin, and Monnie carried her doll in her hood, just the way Koko's mother carried her baby.

For Menie, his father made dog harnesses out of walrus hide. He made them just the right size for Nip and Tup.

Menie harnessed the little dogs to his sled. Then he and Monnie would play sledge journeys. Annadore would sit on the sled all wrapped in furs, while Menie drove the dogs, and Monnie followed after.

Nip and Tup did not like this play very well, and they didn't always go where they were told to. Once they dashed right over the igloo and spilled Annadore off.

Annadore rolled down one side of the igloo, while Nip and Tup galloped down the other. Annadore was buried in the snow and had to be dug out, so it was quite a serious accident, you see, but Nip and Tup did not seem to feel at all responsible about it.

Kesshoo made knives and queer spoons out of bone or ivory for Koolee, and for himself he made new barbs for his bladder-dart, new bone hooks for fishlines, and all sorts of things for hunting.

He made salmon spears, and bird darts, and fishlines, and he ornamented his weapons with little pictures or patterns. He carved two frogs on the handle of his snow knife, and scratched the picture of a walrus on the blade.

Sometimes Koolee carved things, too, but most of the time she was busy making coats or kamiks, or chewing skins to make them soft and fine for use in the igloo; or to cover the kyaks, or to make their summer tent.

Once during the winter the whole family went thirty miles up the coast by moonlight to visit Koolee's brother in another village. They went with the dog sledge, and it took them two days.

They had meat and blubber with them and plenty of warm skins, and when they got tired, Kesshoo made a snow house for them to rest in. The twins thought this was the best fun of all.

II.

When spring came on, there were other things to do. As the days grew longer, the ice in the bay cracked and broke into small pieces and floated away.

The water turned deep blue, and danced in the sunlight, and ice floated about in it. Often there were walrus on these ice-pans.

The twins sometimes saw their huge black bodies on the white ice, and heard their hoarse barks. Then all the men in the village would rush for their kyaks and set out after the walrus.

The men were brave and enjoyed the dangerous sport, but the women used to watch anxiously until they saw the kyaks coming home towing the walrus behind them.

Then they would rush down to the shore, help pull the kyaks up on the beach, where they cut the walrus in pieces and divided it among the families of the hunters.

When the snow had melted on the Big Rock, hundreds of sea-birds made their nests there and filled the air with their cries.

Sometimes Kesshoo went egg hunting on the cliff, and sometimes he set traps there for foxes, and he helped Menie and Koko make a little trap to catch hares. There was plenty to do in every season of the year.

At last the nights shortened to nothing at all. The long day had begun. The stone but, which they had found so comfortable in winter, seemed dark and damp now.

Menie and Monnie remembered the summer days when they did not have to dive down through a hole to get into their house, so Menie said to Monnie one day, "Let's go and ask father if it isn't time to put up the tents."

They ran out to find him. He was down on the beach talking with Koko's father and the other men of the village.

On the beach were two very long boats. The men were looking them over carefully to see if they were water tight.

Koko was with the men. When he saw the twins coming, he tore up the slope to meet them, waving his arms and shouting, "They're getting out the woman-boats! They're getting out the woman-boats!"

This was glorious news to the twins. They ran down to the beach with Koko as fast as their legs could carry them.

They got there just in time to hear Koko's father say to Kesshoo, "I think it's safe to start. The ice is pretty well out of the bay, and the reindeer will be coming down to the fiords after fresh moss."

All the men listened to hear what Kesshoo would say, and the twins listened, too, with all their ears.

"If it's clear, I think we could start after one more sleep," said Kesshoo.

III.

The twins didn't wait to hear any more. They flew for home, and dashed down the tunnel and up into the room.

Koolee was gathering all the knives and spoons and fishing-things and sewing things, and dumping them into a large musk-ox hide which was spread on the floor.

The musk-ox hide covered the entrance hole. The first thing Koolee knew something thumped the musk-ox skin on the under side, and the knives and thimbles and needle cases and other things flew in all directions. Up through the hole popped the faces of Menie and Monnie!

"Oh, Mother," they shouted. "We're going off on the woman-boats! After only one more sleep, if it's pleasant! Father said so!"

Koolee laughed. "I know it!" she said. "I was just packing. You can help me. There's a lot to do to get ready."

The twins were delighted to help. They got together all their own treasures; the sled, and the fishing rods, the dog harnesses, and Annadore, and bound them up with walrus thongs. All but Annadore. Annadore rode in Monnie's hood as usual.

Koolee gathered all her things together again and wrapped them in the musk-ox hide. She took down the long narwhal tusks that the dog harnesses were hung on.

These were the tent poles. She and the twins carried all these things to the beach. The men stayed on the beach and packed the things away in the boats. The other women brought down their bundles from their igloos. There was room for everything in the two big boats.

Only the skins were left on the sleeping bench in the hut. When everything else was ready, Koolee and the twins went up on top of the igloo.

They pulled the moss and dirt out of the chinks between the stones that made the roof, and then Koolee pulled up the stones themselves and let them fall over to one side. This left the roof open to the sky.

"What makes you do that?" Menie asked.

"So the sun and rain can clean house for us," said Koolee.

Everybody else in the village got ready in the same way.

At last Kesshoo came up from the beach and said to Koolee, "Let us have some meat and a sleep and then we will start. Everything is ready. The boats are packed and it looks as if the weather would be clear."

Koolee brought out some walrus meat and blubber for supper, though it might just as well be called breakfast, for there was no night coming, and the twins ate theirs sitting on the roof of the igloo with their feet hanging down inside.

Once Menie's feet kicked his father's head. It was an accident, but Kesshoo reached up and took hold of Menie's foot and pulled him down on to the sleeping bench and rolled him over among the skins.

"Crawl in there and go to sleep," he said.

Monnie let herself down through the roof by her hands and crept in beside Menie. Then Kesshoo and Koolee wrapped themselves in the warm skins and lay down, too.

It took Menie and Monnie some time to go to sleep, for they could look straight up through the roof at the sky, and the sky was bright and blue with little white clouds sailing over it. Besides, they were thinking about the wonderful things that would happen when they should wake up.

CHAPTER IX. THE VOYAGE

I.

When the twins awoke, the sun was shining as brightly as ever, and Nip and Tup were barking at them through the hole in the roof.

Kesshoo and Koolee were gone!

Menie and Monnie were frightened. They were afraid they were left behind. They sat up in bed and howled!

In a moment Koolee's face looked down at them through the roof.

"What's the matter?" she said.

"We thought we were left," wailed Monnie!

"As if I could leave you behind!" cried Koolee.

She laughed at them. "Hand up the skins to me," she said. She reached her arm down the hole and pulled out all the skins from the bed as fast as the twins gave them to her.

Then she put her head down into the opening and looked all around. "We haven't left a thing," she said; "come along."

The twins couldn't climb out through the roof, though they wanted to, so they went out by the tunnel, and helped their mother carry the skins to the beach.

All the people in the village and all the dogs were there before them. The great woman-boats were packed, the kyaks of the men waited beside them in a row on the beach, with their noses in the water.

The dogs barked and raced up and down the beach, the babies crowed, and the children shouted for joy. Even the grown people were gay. They talked in loud tones and laughed and made jokes.

II.

At last Kesshoo shouted, "All ready! In you go!" He told each person where to sit.

He put the Angakok in one boat to steer. He put Koko's father in the other.

In Koko's father's boat he placed Koko and his mother and the baby, Koolee and the twins, the pups, all three dogs, and four of the women who lived in the other igloos. So you see it was quite a large boat.

In the Angakok's boat he placed his two wives, and all the rest of the women and children and dogs. The women took up the paddles. One end of the boat was partly in the water when they got in. The men gently pushed it farther out until it floated.

Then the men got into their kyaks at the water's edge, fastened their skin coats over the rims, and paddled out into deep water.

At last, when all the boats, big and little, were afloat, Kesshoo called out, "We are going north. Follow me."

The women obeyed the signal of Koko's father and the Angakok. The paddles dipped together into the water. The great boats moved! They were off!

The children all sat together in the bottom of the boat, but the twins and Koko were big enough to see over the sides. While the babies played with the dogs, they were busy watching the things that passed on the shores. Soon they passed the Big Rock with little auks and puffins flying about it. They could see the red feet of the puffins, and a blue fox sitting on the top of the rock, waiting for a chance to catch a bird.

Then the Big Rock hid the village from sight.

III.

Beyond the Big Rock the country was all new to the twins and Koko. They looked into narrow bays and inlets as the boat moved along, and saw green moss carpeting the sunny slopes in sheltered places.

They could even see bright flowers growing in the warm spots which faced the sun. The sky was blue overhead. The water was blue below.

Beyond the green slopes they could see the bare hillsides crowned with the white ice cap which never melts, and streams of water dashing down the hillsides and pouring themselves into the waters of the bay.

When they had gone a good many miles up the coast, Kesshoo waved his hand and pointed to a strange sight on the shore.

There was a great river of ice! They could see where it came out of a hollow place between two hills. It looked just like a river, only it was frozen solid, and the end of it, where it came into the sea, was broken off like a great wall of ice, and there were cakes of ice floating about in the water.

Suddenly there was a cracking sound. Menie had heard that sound before. It was the same sound that he had heard when he went seal-hole hunting and got carried away on the ice raft. Menie didn't like the sound anymore. It scared him!

Right after the cracking noise Kesshoo's voice shouted, "Row farther out! Follow me!"

He turned his kyak straight out to sea. All the other boats followed.

They had gone only about half a mile when suddenly there was a loud crick-crick-CRACK as if a piece of the world had broken off, and then there was a splash that could be heard for miles, if there had been any one to hear it.

The end of the glacier, or ice river, had broken off and fallen down into the water! It had made an iceberg!

The splash was so great that in a moment the waves it made reached the boats. The boats rocked up and down on the water and bounced about like corks.

The twins and Koko thought this was great fun, but the Angakok didn't like it a bit. One wave splashed over him, and some of the water went down his neck.

All the grown people knew that if they hadn't rowed quickly away from shore when Kesshoo called they might have been upset and drowned.

IV.

When the waves made by the iceberg had calmed down again, Kesshoo paddled round among the boats.

He said, "I think we'd better land about a mile above here. There's a stream there, and perhaps we can get some salmon for our dinner."

He led the way in his kyak, and all the other boats followed. They kept out of the path of the iceberg, which had already floated some distance from the shore, and it was not long before they came to a little inlet.

Kesshoo paddled into it and up to the very end of it, where a beautiful stream of clear water came dashing down over the rocks into the sea.

The hills sloped suddenly down to the shore. The sun shone brightly on the green slopes, and the high cliffs behind shut off the cold north winds. It was a little piece of summer set right down in the valley.

"Oh, how beautiful!" everybody cried.

The boats were soon drawn up on the beach, the women and children tumbled out, and then began preparations for dinner.

The women got out their cooking pots, and Koolee set to work to make a fireplace out of three stones.

They had blubber and moss with them, but how could they get a fire? They had no matches. They had never even heard of a match.

The Angakok sat down on the beach. He had some little pieces of dry driftwood and some dried moss.

He held one end of a piece of driftwood in a sort of handle which he pressed against his lips. The other end was in a hollow spot in another piece of wood.

The Angakok rolled one driftwood stick round and round in the hollow spot of the other. He did this by means of a bow which he pulled from one side to the other. This made the stick whirl first one way, then back again. Soon a little smoke came curling up round the stick.

Koolee dropped some dried moss on the smoking spot. Suddenly there was a little blaze!

She fed the little flame with more moss, and then lighted the moss on the stones of the fireplace. She put a soapstone kettle filled with water over the fire, and soon the kettle was boiling.

While all this was going on down on the beach, the men took their salmon spears and went up the river, and Koko and the twins went with them.

The wives of the Angakok went to find moss to feed the fire. They brought back great armfuls of it, and put it beside the fireplace.

Koolee was the cook. She stayed on the beach and looked after the babies and the dogs, and the fire. Everything was ready for dinner, except the food!

Meanwhile the men had found a good place where there were big stones in the river. They stood on these stones with their spears in their hands. There were hundreds of salmon in the little stream. The salmon were going up to the little lake from which the river flowed.

When the fish leaped in the water, the men struck at them with their fish spears. There were so many fish, and the men were so skilful that they soon had plenty for dinner.

They strung them all on a walrus line and went back to the beach. Koolee popped as many as she could into her pot to cook, but the men were so hungry they ate theirs raw, and the twins and Koko had as many fishes' eyes to eat as they wanted, for once in their lives.

When everybody had eaten as much as he could possibly hold, the babies were rolled up in furs in the sand and went to sleep. The Angakok lay down on the sand in the sunshine with his hands over his stomach and was soon asleep, too.

The men sat in a little group near by, and Menie and Koko lay on their stomachs beside Kesshoo.

The women had gone a little farther up the beach. The air was still, except for the rippling sound of the water, the distant chatter of the women, the snores of the Angakok, and the buzzing of mosquitoes!

For quite a long time everybody rested. Menie and Koko didn't go to sleep. They were having too much fun. They played with shells and pebbles and watched the mosquitoes buzzing over the Angakok's face. There were a great many mosquitoes, and they seemed to like the Angakok. At last one settled on his nose, and bit and bit. Menie and Koko wanted to slap it, but, of course, they didn't dare. They just had to let it bite!

All of a sudden the Angakok woke up and slapped it himself. He slapped it harder than he intended to. He looked very much surprised and quite offended about it. He sat up and looked round for his wives, as if he thought perhaps they had something to do with it. But they were at the other end of the beach. The Angakok yawned and rubbed his nose, which was a good deal swollen.

Just then Kesshoo spoke, "I think we shall look a long time before we find a better spot than this to camp," he said. "Here are plenty of salmon. We can catch all we need to dry for winter use, right here. There must be deer farther up the fiord. What do you say to setting up the tents right here?"

When Kesshoo said anything, the others were pretty sure to agree, because Kesshoo was such a brave and skillful man that they trusted his judgment.

All the men said, "Yes, let us stay."

Then the Angakok said, "Yes, my children, let us stay! While you thought I was asleep here on the sand I was really in a trance. I thought it best to ask my Tornak about this spot, and whether we should be threatened here by any hidden danger. My Tornak says to stay!"

This settled the matter.

"Tell the women," said Kesshoo. Koko's father went over to the place where the women and children were.

"Get out the tent poles," he called to them. "Here's where we stay."

V.

The women jumped up and ran to the woman-boats. They got out the long narwhal tusks, and the skins, and set them down on the beach.

"Come with me," Koolee called to the twins. She gave them each a long tent pole to carry. She herself carried the longest pole of all, and a pile of skins.

Koolee led the way up the green slope to a level spot overlooking the stream and the bay. It was beside some high rocks, and there were smaller stones all about.

There was a flat stone that she used for the sleeping bench. When the poles were set up and securely fastened, she got the tent skins and covered the poles.

She put on one layer of skin with the hair inside and over that another covering of skin with the fur side out. She sewed the skins together over the entrance with leather thongs and left a flap for a door.

Then she placed stones around the edge of the tent covering to keep the wind from blowing it away. She piled the bed skins on the rock, and their summer house was ready.

The twins brought the musk-ox hides, with all their treasures in them, and the cooking pots and knives and household things from the beach, while Koolee made the fireplace in the tent.

She made the fireplace by driving four sticks into the ground and lashing them together to make a framework. She hung the cooking kettle by straps from the four corners. Under the kettle on a flat stone she placed the lamp. Then the stove was ready.

"We shall cook out of doors most of the time," she said to the twins, "but in rainy weather we shall need the lamp."

It was only a little while before there was a whole new village ready to live in, with plenty of fish and good fresh water right at hand.

VI.

Menie and Monnie were happy in their new home. They climbed about on the rock and found a beautiful cave to play in. They gathered flowers and shells and colored stones and brought them to their mother.

Then later they went for more fish with the men, and Kesshoo let them stand on the stones and try to spear the fish just the way the men did.

Menie caught one, and Koko caught one, but Monnie had no luck at all. "Anyway, I caught a codfish once," Monnie said, to comfort herself.

In two hours everything was as settled about the camp as if they had lived there a week, and every one was hungry again. Hungriness and sleepiness came just as regularly as if they had had nights and clocks both, to measure time by.

When the food was ready, Kesshoo called "Ujo, ujo," which meant "boiled meat," and everybody came running to the beach.

The men sat in one circle, the women and children in another. Pots of boiled fish were set in the middle of the circles, and they all dipped in with their fingers and took what they wanted.

When everybody had eaten, the children played on the beach. They skipped stones and danced and played ball, and their mothers played with them.

The men had their fun, too. They sat in their circle, told stories, and played games which weren't children's games, and the Angakok sang a song, beating time on a little drum. All the men sang the chorus.

By and by, Koolee saw Monnie's head nodding. So she said to the twins, "Come, children, let's go up to the tent."

She took their hands and led them up the slope.

"We're not sleepy," the twins declared.

"I am," said Koolee, "and I want you with me."

They went into the tent, which was not so light as it was out of doors in the bright sunlight. Then they undressed, crawled in among the deerskins, and were soon sound asleep, all three of them. After a while Kesshoo came up from the beach and went to sleep too.

CHAPTER X. THE SUMMER DAY

I.

The summer days flew by, only one really shouldn't say days at all, but summer day. For three whole bright months it was just one daylight picnic all the time!

The people ate when they were hungry and slept when they were sleepy. The men caught hundreds of salmon, and the women split them open and dried them on the rocks for winter use. The children played all day long.

The men hunted deer and musk-ox and bears up in the hills and brought them back to camp. They hunted game both by land and by sea. There was so much to eat that everybody grew fatter, and as for the Angakok, he got so very fat that Koko said to Menie, "I don't believe we can ever get the Angakok home in the woman-boat! He's so heavy he'll sink it! I think it would be a good plan to tie a string to him and tow him back like a walrus!"

"Yes," said Menie. "Maybe he would shrink some if we soaked him well. Don't you know how water shrinks the walrus hide cords that we tie around things when we want them to hold tight together?"

It was lucky for Menie and Koko that nobody heard them say that about the Angakok. It would have been thought very disrespectful.

When the game grew scarce, or they got tired of camping in one spot everything was piled into their boats again, and away they went up the coast until they found another place they liked better. Then they would set up their tents again.

Sometimes they came to other camps and had a good time meeting new people and making new friends.

At last, late in August, the sun slipped down below the edge of the World again. It stayed just long enough to fill the sky with wonderful red and gold sunset clouds, then it came up again. The next night there was a little time between the sunset sky and the lovely colors of the sunrise.

The next night was longer still. Each day grew colder and colder. Still the people lingered in their tents. They did not like to think the pleasant summer was over, and the long night near.

But at last Kesshoo said, "I think it is time to go back to winter quarters. The nights are fast growing longer. The snow may be upon us any day now. I don't know of a better place to settle than the village where we spent last winter. The igloos are all built there ready to use again. What do you say? Shall we go back there?"

"Yes, let us go back," they all said.

II.

The very next day they started. The boats were heavily loaded with dried fish, there were great piles of new skins heaped in the woman-boats, and every kyak towed a seal.

For days they traveled along the coast, stopping only for rest and food. The twins and Koko sat in the bottom of the boat with the dogs, and listened to the regular dip of the paddles, to the cries of the sea-birds as they flew away toward the south, and to the chatter of the women. These were almost the only sounds they heard, for the silence of the Great White World was all about them. They talked together in low voices and planned all the things they would do when the long night was really upon them once more.

When at last they came in sight of the Big Rock, they felt as if they had reached home after a very long journey.

Koko stood up in the boat and pointed to it. "See," he cried, "there's the Big Rock where we found the bear!"

"Yes," Monnie said, "and where we slid downhill."

"And I see where I got caught on the ice raft," Menie shouted.

"Sit down," said Koko's mother. "You'll tip the boat and spill us all into the water."

Koko sat down; the boat glided along through the water, nearer and nearer, until at last they came round the Big Rock, and there, just as if they had not been away at all, lay the whole village of five igloos, looking as if it had gone to sleep in the sunshine.

The big boats waited until the men had all paddled to the shore and beached their kyaks, then they were drawn carefully up on to the sand, and every one got out. The beach at once became a very busy place. The men pulled the walruses and seals out of the water and took care of the boats, while the women set up the tents, cut the meat into big pieces for storage, and carried all their belongings to the tents.

Although the village looked just the same, other things looked quite different. Nip and Tup were big dogs by this time. They ran away up the beach with Tooky and the other dogs the moment they were out of the boats. They did not stay with the twins all the time now, as they used to do. The twins were much bigger, too. Koolee looked at them as they helped her carry the tent-skins up from the beach, and said to them, "My goodness, I must make my needles fly! Winter is upon us and your clothes are getting too small for you! You must have new things right away." The twins thought this was a very good idea. They liked new clothes as well as any one in the world.

Koolee set up the tent beside their old igloo, and there they lived while the men of the village went out every day in their kyaks for seal and walrus, or back into the hills after other game to store away for food during the long winter. The women scraped and cured the skins and cut up the meat and packed it away as fast as the men could kill the game and bring it home.

Each day it grew colder, and each night was longer than the last, until one short September day there came a great snow storm! It snowed all day long, and that night the wind blew so hard that Koolee and the twins nearly froze even among the fur covers of their bed, and when morning came they found themselves nearly buried under a great drift.

That very day Koolee put the stones over the roof of the igloo once more, and the twins helped her fill in the chinks with moss and earth, and cover it with a heavy layer of snow, patted down with the snow shovel, until everything was snug and tight again.

Then they moved in. By the next day all the igloos in the village were in use, and when night came their windows shone with the light of the lamps, just as they had so many months before.

Nip and Tup slept outside with Tooky now, in a snow house which Kesshoo had built for them. Menie and Monnie missed them, but Koolee said, "You are getting so big now you must begin to do something besides play with puppies. Monnie must learn to sew, and Menie must help Father with feeding the dogs and looking after their harnesses, and driving the sledge."

"Maybe Father will teach you both to carve fine things out of ivory this winter! Monnie will soon need her own thimble and needles. They must be made. And she can help me clean the skins and suck out the blubber, and prepare them for being made into clothes!"

"Dear me! what a lot there is to do to keep clothes on our backs and food in our mouths! The Giants are always waiting before the igloo and we must work very hard to keep them outside!"

She did not mean real giants. She meant that Hunger and Want are always waiting to seize the Eskimo who does not work all the time to supply food for himself and his family. She meant that Menie must learn to be a brave strong hunter, afraid of nothing on sea or land, and that Monnie must learn to do a woman's work well, or else the time would come when they would be without food or shelter or clothing, and the fierce cold would soon make an end of them.

It was lucky they got into the warm igloo just when they did, for the winter had come to stay. The bay froze over far out from shore, and the white snow covered the igloos so completely that if it had not been for the windows, and for people moving about out of doors, no one could have told that there was any village there.

The Last Day of all was so short that Menie and Monnie and Koko saw the whole of it from the top of the Big Rock! They had gone up there in the gray twilight that comes before the sunrise to build a snow house to play in. They had been there only a little while when the sky grew all rosy just over the Edge of the World. The color grew stronger and stronger until the little stars were all drowned in it and then up came the great round red face of the sun itself! The children watched it as it peered over the horizon, threw long blue shadows behind them across the snow, and then sank slowly, slowly down again, leaving only the flaming colors in the sky to mark the place where it had been. They waved their hands as it slipped out of sight. "Good bye, old Sun," they shouted, "and good bye, Shadow, too! We shall be glad to see you both when you come back again."

Then, because the wind blew very cold and they could see a snow cloud coming toward them from the Great White World where the Giants lived, the children ran together down the snowy slope toward the bright windows of their homes.

Lucy Fitch Perkins – A Short Biography

One of American literature's almost forgotten names, but in the early 20th Century a wildly popular authoress is Lucy Fitch Perkins, author and illustrator of children's books and originator of the popular Twins series. She was born on 12th July 1865 in Maples, Indiana. Her father, Appleton Howe Fitch, had graduated from Amherst college and spent his professional career working as a teacher and eventually become principle of a school in Chicago. Shortly before his daughter's birth he exchanged teaching for the lumber business and the family relocated to Maples for its forestry. Her mother was Elizabeth Bennett. Both her parents were Puritan, and ensured that a key value in their children's upbringing was education. Though Lucy and her sisters were home-schooled, their parents made sure that they frequently visited Massachusetts and their ancestral home, approximately twenty-five miles out of Boston, where the girls spent time in school so they might experience social interaction with others their age.

Eventually, in 1879, the family permanently removed to the property in Massachusetts, and the girls spent the remainder of their school years here. Lucy displayed early talent in writing and drawing and when she graduated from high school she chose to attend the art school at the Boston Museum of Fine Arts, where she was a student for three years. After graduating, she found employment illustrating for the Prang Educational Company of Boston, where she stayed for a year before moving on to a teaching post at the Pratt Institute, then only recently established.

During these years she made the first inroads into a career in this field, illustrating a translation of The Goose Girl, a German fairy tale made known as Tale no. 89 in the Brothers Grimm's collections, and A Book of Joys: The Story of a New England Summer, which she both wrote and illustrated.

Lucy spent four years working at the Pratt Institute, continuing her own studies while carrying out her teaching duties. She writes of her time there as "happy", enjoying the combination of working on her own talents, while passing them on to others. Then, in 1881, she married a young architect named Dwight Heald Perkins. They had met years earlier while they were both studying in Boston. Their married home was to be in Evanston, Chicago, where Lucy gave birth to Eleanor Ellis and Lawrence Bradford Perkins. They lived here for several years, Lucy working as an illustrator for various publishers and magazines and Dwight as a teacher at the Massachusetts Institute of Technology. They were both active members of their community, and Lucy writes that they "lived fully in the events and thought currents of the time".

She was forty-eight when she was approached by a publisher friend who, aware and impressed by her talents as both an illustrator, which was her profession, and as a writer, which he knew through correspondence, urged her to write. He was so earnest that she thought of an idea for a children's book the next morning, and she immediately set to work making sketches and preparing the idea for presentation. The publisher came to dinner at their house the next evening and she took the opportunity to show him. He responded "go ahead and write it, and I want it". That book was The Dutch Twins, the first in what became a popular series. Using simple language, vivid imagery, stories of adventure and simple moral issues, the stories gently introduced their readers to other countries and cultures, and some of their basic differences with America. Though she had previously published The Goose Girl and A Book of Joys, there is a shift in emphasis from the illustrations to the writing; previously, the illustrations were the primary focus of the books, whereas now, they merely complimented the vividness of her imagery in writing.

Lucy later wrote of the Twins series that they were borne of two key ideas. The first, of "the necessity for mutual respect and understanding between people of different nationalities" if there was ever to be global peace, she felt particularly resonated in her own country, where "all the nations of the earth are represented in the population" (indeed, the term 'melting pot' which we use to describe civilisations where several different cultures are to be found living together was just being coined as a descriptive term in America). The second of these two ideas was that it was possible to hold a child's attention, even when writing about big, complex ideas, so long as the language and story were engaging. As an example, in The Dutch Twins, Lucy touches upon proto-feminist ideas through a childish discussion between her twins about the ships sailing past them as the fish with their grandfather on the dyke near their home.

"I think I'll be a sea captain when I'm big," said Kit.
"So will I,", said Kat.
"Girls can't," said Kit.
But Grandfather shook his head and said: "You can't tell what a girl may be by the time she's four feet and a half high and is called Katrina. There's no telling what girls will do anyway."

This particular interest in Katrina's potential is reflected in Lucy's involvement in several social and artistic reform groups in Chicago, including the Chicago Women's Club and the League of Women Voters.

She saw the need for the themes of each story to be made vivid by their effect on the individuals involved. For Kit and Kat, young siblings growing up together and playing together, witnessing the ships sailing in front of them, the realisation of the female potential is made more vivid than if it were merely being explained to them in a classroom. By witnessing the ships sailing for America, England and elsewhere, Kat sees how the profession of sea-captain is a means for adventure and exploration, and so the injustice of the default, immediate "girls can't" is made painfully apparent. Similarly, to the American children reading the tale, since they can relate to the children's play and childishness, the messages is made more accessible. Lucy writes "I visited a school in Chicago where children of twenty-seven different nationalities were herded in one building, and marveled at what the teachers were able to accomplish. It seemed to me it might help in the fusing process if these children could be interested in the best qualities which they bring to our shores." Over two decades, Lucy wrote 26 stories in the Twins series. The popular children's author Beverly Cleary notes that the Twins series engaged her as an early reader, and ultimately served as inspiration for her writing. Alongside the Twins series, Lucy illustrated Edith Ogden Harrison's fairy tales, which were published in the 1900s.

As she well understood, it remains important to teach children early of the value of other cultures, and the history of one's own. Her writing can still be used as effective learning tools for their playful language, humour clarity still engages a young audience. Moreover, the sketches afford a visual representation of clothing and thereby a subtle hint at costume design for those children so enamoured with the stories that they wish to act them out. The Irish Twins, in particular, addresses "the abuses of absentee landlordism" which partly caused the mass immigration from Ireland to America at the country's birth.

Lucy died while holidaying in Pasadena, California, on 18th March 1937. She was seventy-two. Her books have been translated into several international languages, for their cultural importance is borderless. She writes that she "tried to contribute something to the making of Americans by an appreciation of what has been done in the past to make America what it is today, and of the constructive qualities in the material at hand with which we must build the nation of the future." This altruism and desire for social and cultural awareness and reform survives her, and though America went though almost a century of widespread social oppression, racism and xenophobia, as new writers and activists seek reform, we would do well to reflect on the pertinence and relevance of Perkins's work.

www.ingramcontent.com/pod-product-compliance
Lightning Source LLC
Chambersburg PA
CBHW061459170626
46811CB00004B/1581